This book is due for return on or before the last date shown below.

10 APR 2023

18 JUL 2023

Titles in Monster Island:

THE APE
TIM COLLINS & ABBY RYDER

THE DINOSAUR
TIM COLLINS & JAMES LAWRENCE

THE SQUID
TIM COLLINS & JAMES LAWRENCE

THE YETI
TIM COLLINS & ABBY RYDER

THE CRAB
TIM COLLINS & JAMES LAWRENCE

THE CYCLOPS
TIM COLLINS & ABBY RYDER

Badger Publishing Limited, Oldmedow Road,
Hardwick Industrial Estate, King's Lynn PE30 4JJ

Telephone: 01438 791037
www.badgerlearning.co.uk

The Ape ISBN 978-1-78837-346-3

2 4 6 8 10 9 7 5 3 1

Publisher / Senior Editor: Danny Pearson
Editor: Claire Morgan
Series Consultant: Dee Reid
Designer: Fiona Grant
Cover Illustration: Mark Penman
Illustration: Abby Ryder

THE APE

Tim Collins

Illustrated by Abby Ryder

Contents

Story Vocabulary
answer
ledge
scratched

4

The story so far...

Imran was stuck on the island. It was very foggy.

"Welcome to Monster Island," said a man. "I am the Captain. You will never escape."

Imran was scared. He thought the Captain was strange.

"Why is it called Monster Island?" asked Imran.

"You will soon find out," said the Captain.

Chapter 1

The Climb

Imran could not see anything.

The fog was too thick.

I must get away from Monster Island, thought Imran. *I will climb a hill to get above the fog.*

Imran climbed and climbed.

But the fog got thicker and thicker.

Then Imran heard someone laughing.

It was the Captain.

"It's not safe up here," said the Captain.

"Why?" asked Imran.

But the Captain didn't answer.

Then Imran heard an angry roar.

It was getting louder and louder.

A giant ape ran out of the fog.

It was coming to get Imran.

Chapter 2

The Chase

The giant ape grabbed Imran with its sharp nails.

It ripped the skin on his arm.

Blood dripped out.

The monster tried to drag Imran away.

Imran picked up a rock.

He hit the monster in the face as hard as he could.

The monster ape roared.

"Big mistake," said the Captain. "Now you have made him really angry."

Imran ran away as fast as he could.

The monster ran after him.

Imran couldn't see where he was going.

The fog was too thick.

The monster was closing in on Imran.

Then Imran came to the edge of a cliff.

It was too far to jump to the other side.

The Captain was standing on the other side of the cliff.

"Help me!" called Imran.

The Captain just laughed.

"Jump across," said the Captain.

Imran looked down.

It was a very long way down.

If he fell, he would die.

But the monster would kill him if he stayed where he was.

Imran jumped.

Chapter 3

The Drop

Imran landed on a ledge just below the far edge of the cliff.

He looked up and saw a huge dark
shape falling over the edge of the cliff.

It was the monster.

The monster tried to grab Imran as it fell.

Its sharp nails scratched Imran's face,
but it did not stop falling.

The monster roared and roared all the way down to the ground.

Then Imran heard a loud thud and the roaring stopped.

Imran had got away from the monster but blood was coming from his arm and his face.

And he was still stuck on the island.

Questions

Chapter 1

What does the Captain tell Imran?
(page 10)

What comes to get Imran? *(page 12)*

Chapter 2

What happens when the monster grabs Imran? *(page 14)*

Why does Imran not want to jump across to the other side? *(page 20)*

Chapter 3

What happens to the monster? *(page 23)*

Do you think Imran will escape from Monster Island?

About the Author

Tim Collins has written over 70 books for children and adults.

He lives near Oxford and spends his time listening to rock music and playing Pokémon.

He went to a real desert island once, but he didn't see any monsters.

About the Illustrator

Abby Ryder is a cartoonist who loves comic books and video games.

She hopes to one day become best friends with a giant robot.